CUP

For Zachary Caleb Tillett
– perhaps one day you'll see England win
the World Cup again!

While this book is based on real characters and actual historical events, some situations and people are fictional, created by the author.

Scholastic Children's Books
Euston House,
24 Eversholt Street
London, NW1 1DB, UK

A division of Scholastic Ltd
London ~ New York ~ Toronto ~ Sydney ~ Auckland
Mexico City ~ New Delhi ~ Hong Kong

First published in the UK by Scholastic Ltd, 2016

ISBN 978 1407 16576 9

Printed and bound by CPI Group (UK) Ltd, Croydon, CR0 4YY

1 3 5 7 9 10 8 6 4 2

WORLD CUP FINAL

TONY BRADMAN

SCHOLASTIC

CHAPTER ONE

'Oh for heaven's sake, Gary, will you please stop looking out of that blasted window!', said Mum. 'I might lose my temper if I have to tell you again.'

'Sorry, Mum,' I said, and quickly sat down on the settee. I tried to concentrate on the television, but it was too hard. My eyes kept drifting back to the window. 'Come on, Dad,' I murmured under my breath. 'They'll be kicking off soon…'

'I don't know why you're bothering anyway,' Mum muttered. She was sitting in one of the front room's two armchairs. 'Your father is bound to be late – if he appears at all, that is. He's never been very good at keeping his promises, has he?'

I opened my mouth to argue with her, but then thought better of it. I didn't understand why Mum was saying she might lose her temper – I thought she was pretty grumpy already. She had kicked Dad out of the house last month, and Susan and I had only seen him twice since then, when he'd taken us to the park on a couple of Saturday mornings. We'd spoken to him on the phone a few times, but we hadn't actually seen him for quite a while. Now he would be spending the whole evening with us, and I was really looking forward to it. I had a feeling Mum wasn't, though. She seemed nervous – but then I don't think she and Dad had spoken more than a few words to each other since the big bust-up.

There are four of us in our family, the Thomsons: Mum, Dad, my younger sister Susan and me. Mum and Dad are both tall – Mum has blonde hair and Dad is dark. Susan and I both have dark hair like him, but we also look like Mum (Susan more than me). They're younger than most of my mates' parents as well – they like nice clothes and they're both fans of The Beatles.

I'd always thought we were happy. Mum and Dad sometimes had rows, like most parents, but recently the rows had got worse. Then one day Mum had said Dad was leaving.

He was miserable, Mum was upset and Susan kept bursting into tears – she is only eight, after all. Of course I was upset too, although I'd tried to keep that to myself. But there was another problem to worry about, something very important – at least as far as I was concerned. This was the summer of 1966 – the World Cup was about to start, and I wanted to watch it with my dad.

I've always been football crazy – I love playing the game, and watching it as well. Dad feels the same, so he's always taken me to see our local team – Crystal Palace, pride of South London – and he comes to watch me play for my school. We're both England supporters, and we'd been looking forward to the World Cup for as long as I could remember – England playing at home, sixteen teams, the world's greatest players, most of the matches on the telly – I mean,

I couldn't think of anything more exciting. Dad even bought a new TV set for the tournament. Everyone we know rents their TV from a shop, but Dad said we could do better than that.

So I'd asked Mum if she'd let Dad come round to watch it with me. It had taken a week of begging and pleading and offering to do jobs around the house until I finally wore her down and she gave in. Tonight was the opening match: England playing Uruguay at Wembley. The teams had marched out, there had been bands and speeches, the Queen had met all the players… but still no Dad.

I knew it would take him a while to get to the house. He didn't finish work at the factory until 4.30pm, and then he would have to clean up and change his clothes. He was living with my Nan and Grandad and their flat was in Lewisham, a couple of bus rides from our estate in Penge. But he'd promised he would definitely be with me for the whole match. *Please don't let me down, Dad,* I thought, and crossed my fingers on both hands…

Then I heard the front gate creak open and footsteps on the path. I was off that sofa faster than Jimmy Greaves to a loose ball in the penalty area, and I opened the front door before Dad had a chance to ring the bell. He stood there grinning at me.

'You going to let me in, or what?' he said. 'We've got a game to watch.'

I grinned back at him, but was barged aside before I could say anything. Susan had come running down the stairs from her bedroom, and she flung her arms around Dad on the doorstep.

'Daddy!' she squealed. 'I've missed you so much!'

'I've missed you too, sweetheart,' Dad said quietly, hugging her tightly in return.

I looked round and saw that Mum had also come out of the front room. She was standing in the hall behind us with her arms folded tightly and a cross look on her face. The kind of look that would have sent most people running for cover.

'Hello, Barbara,' Dad said, and for a few seconds they stared at each other. I looked at Susan and she looked at me, her eyes wide. It felt like a very tense moment.

Mum then turned on her heels and strode off into the kitchen, where she started clattering about. I dragged Dad into the front room, just in time for the kick-off, and we settled down to watch the game. Not that it was much good. All right then, I'll admit it was, well… dull. England worked their socks off, but they couldn't break through

Uruguay's defence. The match ended in a nil-nil draw, and the Wembley crowd booed as the teams left the pitch.

'What do you think, Dad?' I said gloomily. I felt like a burst balloon. After all the waiting and the build-up, the game had been a huge disappointment. 'I can't see us winning the

Cup if we keep playing like that. We should have thrashed them.'

'Oh, I don't know,' said Dad. He was sitting on the settee with Susan and I snuggled next to him. 'The lads were probably nervous, and South American teams can be hard to score against. Greaves played well, though...'

'He still didn't score though, did he?' I said. 'He usually gets a hat-trick—'

'Right, I think you'd better go now, Mike,' interrupted Mum, coming into the front room. 'It's late and the kids should be in bed. They've got school in the morning.'

Dad frowned, and for a moment I thought there was going to be another row. But he shrugged instead and nodded. 'Fair enough,' he said, and stood up to leave.

'Can Dad come for the next game?' I asked, looking at Mum. We were playing Mexico on Saturday, and after tonight's draw it was vital that we win.

Now it was Mum's turn to shrug. 'I suppose so,' she said. But she didn't seem happy about it.

Susan and I said our goodbyes to Dad in the hall. He didn't look happy either, and Susan was sniffling. I have to say I felt a bit tearful too as I watched Dad trudge off into the night. But I didn't cry, even though it had turned out to be a miserable evening. Instead I found myself thinking I would do anything to get Mum and Dad back together.

But it didn't look very likely at that moment, did it?

CHAPTER TWO

I was still brooding the next morning on my paper round. The newsagent I work for is called Mr Challis, and he's a nice man, always laughing and joking even though he has to get up really early to sort out the newspapers for delivery. I get up early every day too, usually at six o'clock – my round takes well over an hour and I have to set off for school with Susan by quarter past eight at the latest.

Most of my mates think I'm mad to do it, but I like earning some money. Mr Challis pays me ten shillings a week and I get tips sometimes as well. I always try to save part of what I earn 'for a rainy day', as Grandad says – it's hard, as I'd much rather spend it, but you never know when you might need a few bob extra. I keep my savings in a piggy bank near my bed. Last time I counted the coins – and the few notes – I had nearly eight pounds.

'Cheer up, Gary!' said Mr Challis as I picked up the bag of newspapers. 'Just be grateful we didn't lose last night. If you ask me, we can only get better!'

I smiled, but I wasn't feeling particularly cheerful as I rode away on my bike. I was worried about the football, of course, but I had other things on my mind too.

What were Mum and Dad playing at? Things could be great for us if they just sorted themselves out. Both Mum and Dad had decent jobs – Dad had done loads of different things, but now he had a new job at an electronics factory. Mum had gone back to work as a filing clerk when Susan had started school. We had a modern council house, and a little while before he'd moved out Dad had even been talking about buying a car.

But that wasn't going to happen, not for the time being anyway. For some reason

Mum and Dad were strapped for cash at the moment. Then I began to wonder if they might actually get divorced. I knew people did – the parents of a girl called Hazel in my class had done just that only last year. But I really didn't like thinking about it much, so I concentrated on finishing my round as quickly as possible. If I let myself, I would probably end up brooding about it all day.

I got home in time to eat a bowl of Rice Krispies, and then I set off for school with Susan. Mum came with us as far as the bus stop on the corner of our road.

'See you later, kids,' she said, and kissed Susan. I ducked out of the way before she could do the same to me. 'And make sure you behave yourselves today...'

That's a bit unfair, I thought. Susan is known for being a good girl at school, and I never misbehave either. I don't find the lessons hard and most of the teachers are okay. I'm ten, so I'm in the third year of the Juniors, and my teacher is Mr Smith. He can be strict but he can also be funny. He likes to read us stories, and our class book this year has been a terrific adventure story called *The Hobbit*. It's full of magic and strange creatures like goblins and dragons, and there are loads of battles too.

My best friends are Colin Jones and John Hawkins. At playtimes we always play football with the other lads, dodging round the girls and their skipping ropes and sometimes getting into arguments with them. We probably look a bit of an odd bunch when we're together – Colin is skinny and has a crew cut, but he's dead nippy with a ball. John is fair-haired and quite plump, but he's a pretty good footballer too.

They're always a bit scruffy, even when

they're wearing school uniform. Mum wouldn't let me get away with being a scruff, though. She makes sure my uniform is always clean and ironed, and she buys me nice clothes for outside school. I was the first one of my mates to get a pair of blue jeans, just like the ones cowboys wear in the films. Everyone at school was dead jealous.

'And it's Bobby Charlton racing through the middle,' Colin announced in his best commentator impression as he dribbled our plastic ball past a couple of defenders. 'He beats the tackle… and shoots!'

We each had our favourites among the England players. Colin was a fan of Bobby Charlton, who played for Manchester United, and John thought Jimmy Greaves of Tottenham Hotspur could do no wrong. But my hero was Bobby Moore, the captain of West Ham and England. He played in the centre of defence and Dad said he was as solid as a rock.

'Fancy a kick-around in the park after school?' John asked at lunchtime.

That was something we often did. Mum didn't get out of the office until five most days. Susan was looked after by Mum's mum, our other Nan, and Mum picked her up on her way home. I had my own key to the house but I liked staying out so I could play with my mates. I mean, there wasn't much to do at home on my own, was there? I liked watching television, but the children's programmes were only on for an hour or so.

The park was empty when Colin, John and I got there. We played for a while which was loads of fun, taking it in turns as goalie, defender and attacker and pretending to be our heroes. Suddenly a little black dog appeared out of nowhere and joined in, chasing the ball and yapping, making it impossible for us to play. Eventually we gave up and looked round for the dog's owner, but there was nobody to be seen.

'It must have got lost,' said Colin, stroking him. The dog wagged his tail happily.

'We should take him home,' said John. 'I wonder where he lives?'

'There's a tag on his collar, I said, and knelt down to read it.

The little dog clambered all over me. He kept trying to lick my face so it was hard to see what it said, but I managed it in the end. 'It says his name is Scruffy,' I read out, 'and that he belongs to… Billy Jackson.'

Colin and John instantly backed away from me and the little dog, their eyes wide with terror. We all knew of the Jacksons – they were the roughest, toughest family on the whole estate. They were dead dodgy, involved in all sorts of stuff, and nearly everyone steered well clear of them. There seemed to be at least half a dozen brothers, most of them in and out of Brixton prison as if it had a revolving door. Billy was twenty or so, and he was definitely trouble – he was big and hard and scary.

'Er… you two can take his dog home if you want,' said Colin. 'I'm off.'

'Me too,' added John. 'The dog will find

his own way home if we leave him.'

'What if he doesn't?' I said. But it was too late. My mates were already running towards the park gates as if they were being chased by a horde of goblins from *The Hobbit*. 'Cheers, lads!' I called crossly as I watched them go. Maybe they were right, too, I told myself. Maybe the little dog would be fine if I abandoned him and went home.

Scruffy was looking at me with his big brown eyes, though. He licked my hand and whined softly, as if he'd just realized he was lost. And that I was a complete softy.

'Come on then,' I sighed. 'I only hope I don't end up regretting this.'

I almost felt as if I were going to an execution.

Mine, probably.

CHAPTER THREE

Of course I had no lead for Scruffy, so I had to carry him all the way. He seemed to enjoy that, and I didn't mind either. He was only a skinny little mongrel, so he wasn't heavy, and the Jackson house wasn't far from the park. It was easy to spot, too – the burnt-out old car in the front garden was a dead giveaway. Scruffy stayed very still in my arms until we got to his front gate. Then he started yapping again, almost as if he wanted to let everyone know he had returned at last from his travels.

I knocked and the front door of the house instantly flew open.

Billy Jackson came running out and loomed over me. He was tall and broad-shouldered, and he had a face that looked as if it had been carved from a lump of rock, although not very well. His ginger hair was cut short, and he was wearing shiny black boots and dark blue Levi jeans held up with red braces over a crisp white Ben Sherman button-down-collar shirt. I was a bit surprised – I hadn't been expecting him to look quite so smart.

'What are you doin' with my dog?' he snarled. His face was so close to mine our noses were almost touching. Scruffy whined with pleasure and licked him.

'Er… I found him in the park,' I said, my voice squeaky with fear. 'I could tell he was lost, so I read his tag and I thought I'd better bring him back to you…'

Billy Jackson frowned, his eyebrows coming together like a pair of hairy ginger caterpillars whispering to each other. Then he grinned and took Scruffy in one of his huge hands. 'Cheers, mate!' he said, and slapped me on the back so hard with his other hand I nearly fell over. 'You'd better come in and have a cuppa or something,' he added, and he dragged me into the house before I had a chance to escape.

'Mum! Dad!' he yelled. 'Some kid's found

Scruffy and brought him home!'

The house was the same as mine – they were all the same on the estate – but it looked very different on the inside. My mum likes nice, proper furniture and she insists on the house always being kept tidy. She often gives me a hard time about the state of my bedroom. I find it annoying, but even I wouldn't want our house to be like the Jackson place. It really was a bit of a mess. The furniture was old and tatty, all the rooms looked as if they needed decorating, and there were lots of cardboard boxes full of stuff piled on top of each other. I had a sneaking suspicion that most of it might have been nicked from somewhere.

Billy's brothers weren't in (which I was quite glad about), but his mum and dad were sitting in the kitchen and they turned out to be nice. Billy looked like his mum, so I suppose most people might think she was scary too. But she smiled a lot, and she made me a cup of tea and gave me a couple of slices of cake.

Billy's dad was dark, wiry and smaller than the other two, and I couldn't help thinking he had a face like a ferret. Or maybe a rat, I couldn't decide.

'You're such a good lad for bringing Scruffy home,' said Mrs Jackson. 'He vanished after lunch, and Billy just couldn't find him anywhere, could you, love?'

'No, I couldn't – bloomin' dog, running off like that...' said Billy, sounding dead annoyed. But I could see just how pleased he was to have Scruffy back.

'Yeah, well, you're a bit of a disappointment, Scruffy,' said Mrs Jackson. 'You could at least have come home with the World Cup, like that Pickles.'

We all laughed. Mrs Jackson was talking about the Jules Rimet Trophy, the actual World Cup itself. It had been put on display in London before the tournament had begun and somebody had stolen it. There had been a nationwide police search, but the trophy was found under a bush by a dog called Pickles, out for a walk with his owner. The story had been all over the papers and on the television news.

'Most people round here think you was the bloke who nicked it in the first place, Dad,' said Billy. He winked at his mum, who grinned and winked back.

'Not guilty, son,' said Mr Jackson, holding his hands up. 'It's a mug's game, nicking stuff like that. Almost impossible to sell, not unless you've got a specialist buyer already lined up. No, I'll stick to what I'm good at, thanks very much…'

We continued talking for a while, but then I realized it was getting late and I said I ought to be going home.

'Thanks again, mate,' said Billy as he

showed me out, Scruffy scampering along behind him, yapping. Billy slapped me on the back once more. 'I definitely owe you,' he added. 'So if you ever need any kind of favour… you only have to ask.'

'Er… okay,' I replied. Why would I ever need a favour from someone like Billy Jackson? It seemed a crazy idea. Our lives were totally different.

Although it turned out not to be quite as crazy as I thought.

Dad did come round on Saturday, and we watched the game together. Alf Ramsey, the England manager, made a couple of changes to the team, in particular bringing in Martin Peters, a young West Ham player everyone had been talking about last season – I thought he was pretty good. Like Uruguay, Mexico were tough to play. But this time our lads were clearly determined to do better. It wasn't until nearly half-time that we scored, but what a goal it was – a Bobby Charlton screamer from twenty-five yards! Dad and I leapt off the settee and hugged each other as if all our Christmases had come at once.

Roger Hunt added a second goal a few minutes later, so it was a FANTASTIC night. Even Mum seemed quite pleased.

The last game in our group was against France the following Wednesday evening, and that mostly went well too. We beat them two-nil, with Roger Hunt scoring both goals. We ended up as clear winners of our group!

I was so pleased I didn't know what to do with myself. The only bad thing was that a French defender hacked down Jimmy Greaves and he had to be carried off. There was blood pouring from his calf and he needed stitches.

'Ouch!' said Dad. 'That could mean he won't make the final.' I knew Dad was right – there might not be enough time for Jimmy Greaves to recover. The final was less than two weeks away.

'Do you really think we can go all the way now, Dad?'

'I'd put money on it. And I tell you

what… if we do, then I'll get us a couple of tickets to Wembley for the big day. That'll be something to remember!'

'Are you serious, Dad?' I jumped off the settee and stood in front of him. I was pretty sure this was the most exciting thing I had ever heard.

'It's a promise, son. Now I think it's time I was on my way…'

When I went to bed that night all I could think about was Dad's promise. It would be incredible to go to the World Cup Final with him and see England win…

CHAPTER FOUR

Mum, however, wasn't impressed by the news at all.

'Your father told you he'd do what?' she said, with a cross look on her face.

It was after tea the next day. Mum had made sausages, chips and beans – one of my favourite meals – and now I was helping her with the washing-up. Susan had gone to play in her room, and I had just been chatting to Mum about stuff in general. Then I had casually dropped Dad's promise into the conversation, hoping to show her what a great bloke he was. But I was beginning to realize that might have been a mistake.

'Er... he told me he would get a couple of tickets to the final...' I muttered.

'Oh, did he, now?' Mum took her hands out of the washing-up bowl, peeled off her yellow rubber gloves, and threw them down on the draining board. 'Typical!' she snorted. Then she stood staring out of the window at our tiny little garden.

'Come on, Mum, don't be hard on him,'

I said. 'I'm sure he'll keep his—'

'His promise?' she snapped, whipping round to look at me. 'You know what I think about your dad's promises, Gary. They're the reason he doesn't live with us.'

'I thought it was because you didn't, well… love him any more.'

I mean, I don't really understand any of that grown-up stuff and what it means, but I'd heard someone on Coronation Street say something similar, and I wondered if it was the way Mum felt.

'Oh, Gary, of course I still love your father,' Mum said quietly, her shoulders slumping. 'But I certainly don't like him much when he makes promises he can't keep, and he does it a lot. It's not fair on me, you or your sister and it's no way to build a life.'

'That's the way he is, though, isn't it? He's always been the same.'

'You're right,' said Mum, shrugging. 'I knew what he was like when I married him, and it didn't matter when we were younger. But now I want a better life for you and your sister, and that won't be easy if your dad just works in a factory. He was always promising me he'd go to night school, take some exams, then get a well-paid office job in a good company and make something of himself...'

Mum turned away from me, and for a moment I thought she might start crying. I didn't know where to look, and for a minute I thought I might start crying too. 'Are you all right, Mum?' I said at last. 'Please, I hate it when you get upset...'

Mum pulled me to her and gave me a hug. 'I'm sorry, Gary,' she said, her voice softer now. 'Perhaps I shouldn't be talking to you like this, but I think you deserve to know what's behind everything that's happened.

Your dad is a good man, and I'm sure he means it when the words come out of his mouth. But he makes promises too quickly without thinking and then gives up on them. I've had enough of that.'

I could understand what Mum was saying. Perhaps I shouldn't have been so keen to believe what Dad had said. Now that I thought about it, I remembered him making quite a few promises in the past that he hadn't kept. It hadn't really bothered me much at the time. Kids often break promises, and I suppose I'd assumed grown-ups did too. It was clearly a bigger problem between adults, though, especially when they were married to each other. Then suddenly a new thought occurred to me, and I felt excited all over again. The answer to our problem was obvious!

'Would you take Dad back if he started keeping his promises?' I asked.

'Of course I would!' Mum gave me a sad smile. 'I'd take him back if he just kept one.' Then she sighed and turned to look out of the window again. 'I'm not going to count on it, though,' she added. 'And I don't think you should either, Gary.'

Suddenly I began to wonder if it might be time to check up on Dad…

I could hardly sleep that night for thinking about what Mum had said. It seemed there was definitely a chance my parents might get back together, but that depended on a couple of big things. First, England had to make it into the World Cup Final. Then Dad had to keep his promise to get a couple of tickets for the match. I kept tossing and turning, worrying that neither of those things would happen.

England hadn't started well, but we had improved, and some of the teams who could have been a threat to us had been knocked out. Brazil were on their way home even though they had Pelé, the world's best player, and they'd won the World Cup in 1962. Italy had been beaten by North Korea, which had shocked everyone, including the North Koreans probably. But Greaves might be out for the rest of the tournament, and there were still some terrific teams who stood between us and the final.

Dad was more of a worry, though. If we didn't get to the final, then it didn't matter if he kept his promise or not as we wouldn't need any tickets. But if we did, keeping his promise was more important than he might realize. It could bring our family back together, and I wanted that even more than I wanted England to win the World Cup. Both would be nice, but I'd settle for one. Could Dad do it? I had a nasty feeling it might be harder to get hold of tickets for the final than he might imagine…

I went to see him after school the next day. It was the last day of the summer term, and there was loads going on, what with the fourth year leaving for good before they went on to secondary school in the autumn, so we still didn't finish till quarter to four. Dad's factory is in Catford, but it didn't take long to get there on my bike. I had a football with me and I waited by the gates for the hooter to blast at 4.30pm.

As everyone came out I spotted Dad and rushed over. Understandably, he was pretty surprised to see me.

'What are you doing here?' he asked, frowning. 'Everything okay at home?'

'Yeah,' I said. 'I just wondered if you wanted to go for a kick-around?'

'Why not?' Dad said with a grin, and we headed for the nearest park.

It was empty, and we ran about in the late-afternoon sun trying to beat each other. Dad used to be a good player himself, but I don't think he's as fit as he was once.

'That's it, I'm shattered!' he said after a while and collapsed panting on the grass. 'You're too good for me, Gary. You'll be playing for England yourself soon.'

I sat down next to him, and we talked. He asked me lots of questions about Mum, and you wouldn't have to be a genius to guess that he badly wanted her to take him back. I thought about telling him that Mum had said she would if he kept just one promise, but decided against it. I didn't want to put him under any pressure – that might make things worse. Besides, I was hoping he had things under control.

'So, Dad, I wanted to ask you…' I said eventually, trying to keep my voice dead calm and casual. 'Have you found out how to get those tickets for the final?'

'Oh, plenty of time for that,' said Dad with a smile and a shrug, as if it couldn't possibly be a problem. 'I'll think about it after the semi. We've got a tough enough game in the quarter-final. Argentina will be no pushover…'

Not the right answer, Dad, I thought, frustrated. Not the right answer at all.

CHAPTER FIVE

The next day was Saturday, which meant I could have a lie-in. I only do my paper round on weekdays, as Mr Challis has a completely different bunch of lads for the weekends. I still went down to his shop later that morning, though. I wanted to ask him how Dad could get two tickets for the final. Mr Challis knows about all sorts of stuff, and I was pretty sure he would know about this as well. I was right, too.

Mr Challis is pretty old – well over fifty at least – and he is almost totally bald. He was standing in his usual place behind the counter. Newspapers and magazines were heaped on it, and behind him the shelves were lined with packets of cigarettes and large jars of sweets.

'Well, if your dad had been quicker off the mark he could have applied for some tickets by post,' he said. 'It's a bit late now – the final is a week today.'

I hadn't thought about that, but he was right. The clock was definitely ticking. 'So what do we do?' I said. 'Isn't there somewhere we can go to buy the tickets?'

'Oh, yes,' said Mr Challis, smiling. 'You could just go to the ticket office at Wembley Stadium. Apparently there are still quite a few tickets left.'

'Really?' My voice was squeaky with a mixture of relief and surprise.

'But they won't last long,' said Mr Challis. 'Especially if we win this afternoon. If I were you, I'd tell your dad to get to Wembley pretty sharpish on Monday…'

It sounded like good advice, but I knew I'd have to pick my moment to raise the subject with Dad. I didn't think it would be the best idea to talk about the tickets in front of Mum – for all I knew it might start them arguing again.

At least Dad was on time. The quarter-final game against Argentina was due to kick off at three o'clock, and he arrived when he said he would, dead on half-past two. There was another surprise – Mum was actually quite nice to him.

'Hello, Mike,' she said, giving him a smile. 'Would you like some tea?'

'Er… I don't mind if I do, Barbara,' Dad replied slowly. Judging by the look on his face he thought it might be a trick question, but it wasn't. Mum made him a cup of tea, just the way he'd always liked it – strong and with three sugars.

'There's cake as well,' she said, bringing everything into the front room on a tray. 'I made a sponge especially for the occasion. This is an important game, isn't it?'

'Oh, yes,' Dad and I said together. 'It's going to be tough, too,' Dad added.

'Well then, perhaps I'll watch it with you,' said Mum. 'Cake, everybody?'

Susan and I exchanged a glance and I shrugged. It was strange for all four of us to be together in one room, drinking tea and eating cake in front of the television like a happy family. I wondered if it had been my conversation with Mum that had made her change her tune. Not that I cared much about the reason. I was pleased, and for the first time since Dad had left I found myself beginning to feel some hope.

I was a lot more nervous about the game, to be honest. Alf Ramsey had made a few changes to the team again, bringing in Everton's Alan Ball, a very good midfield player, and yet another West Ham player, the striker Geoff Hurst. He had been the top scorer in the First Division last season. But Argentina were supposed to be one of the best teams in the tournament, and they had done pretty well in their group.

'We don't have any wingers, either,' I said. 'I don't understand why.'

'It's this new way Ramsey wants to play, four-four-two,' said Dad. 'Four at the back, four across the midfield, and two strikers up front. He reckons it's the best system for the players he's got, and that it works better than having wingers.'

'Well, we'll soon see, I suppose,' I said, but I wasn't sure, and I knew I wasn't the only one.

I had read all the sports pages in the newspapers I delivered and I'd seen a lot of criticism of the England manager's tactics. Some people thought he was making the team boring – they hadn't exactly been playing spectacular football. But others said it was only the results that counted, and I probably agreed.

I thought the team seemed strong – Gordon Banks in goal, George Cohen and Ray Wilson as full-backs, Jack Charlton next to Bobby Moore in the centre of the back four. Nobby Stiles played in front of them – people always commented on how he looked (he was short and missing his front teeth), but he was a terrific tackler. Martin Peters, Alan Ball and Bobby Charlton (Jack's brother) completed the midfield. That left Roger Hunt and Geoff Hurst as our strikers.

Even so, I was on the edge of my seat when the game kicked off. Argentina looked good on the ball, but they had a reputation for being rough too, and they certainly put in some tough tackles.

'The ref is going to have to stay on top of that,' Dad muttered. It almost seemed as if the referee heard him – in that moment he booked the Argentine captain Antonio Rattin for a foul on Bobby Charlton.

Things went from bad to worse after that. There were some nasty tackles and the whole game seemed very bad-tempered. Antonio Rattin argued with the referee about every decision that went against his team. At last the referee snapped and sent him off. But Rattin refused to leave the field, and it looked as if the referee might even have to abandon the game. Dad and I were yelling at the telly, and the Wembley crowd was going mad, booing and whistling. Rattin went eventually, although he had to be escorted away by two policemen, and he argued with the crowd as he left.

And that was only the first half! The second half wasn't quite so dramatic, but it was just as nerve-wracking. Argentina still looked capable of beating us even though they were down to ten men – and this was the knock-out stage, so we would be out of the tournament if we lost. I think I nearly chewed my fingernails down to the bone. When Geoff Hurst scored not long before the end we exploded with relief.

One-nil to England! 'Phew, that was close!' Dad said when the whistle went at last for full time. We were in the semi-finals, the last four in the World Cup!

I sat there in a daze, thinking about it. This was the furthest any England team had ever got in the World Cup, and we were now only one match away – one match! – from the final. Then I remembered I wanted to talk to Dad about the tickets. That turned out to be impossible though. He stayed for quite a while longer, but spent most of the time talking to Susan so I didn't get a chance to catch him on his own.

That night I dreamed Dad found a couple of finals tickets under a bush in the park. But just as he reached down to pick them up, the wind blew them away...

I woke up in a cold sweat, and couldn't go back to sleep, no matter how hard I tried.

CHAPTER SIX

Over the next few days the papers were full of the story of Antonio Rattin's sending-off, and it was talked about on the television a lot too. In the press conference after the game Alf Ramsey said the Argentines had behaved like 'animals', and of course that made them very angry. Some of the South Americans said it had all been a fix, that the referee had been bribed to send Rattin off so England would win.

'That's utter rubbish,' snorted Mr Challis on Monday morning. 'They spoiled a good game with their tactics, and we deserved to win. They're just bad losers.'

'It's strange though, isn't it?' I said. 'The South American teams were supposed to be the best in the world, but none of them have made it through to the semi-finals, have they?'

The other three quarter-finals had all been won by European teams as well. West Germany beat Uruguay four-nil, and two of the Uruguayans had been sent off. North Korea had gone three-nil up in the first half of their game against Portugal, but the Portuguese had made it a real thriller with an amazing comeback, scoring five goals to win five-three. And the Soviet Union had beaten Hungary two-one.

'I don't think it's strange at all – the best teams got through,' said Mr Challis. 'By the way, has your dad done anything about getting hold of those tickets?'

'Er… I don't think so,' I said. 'I'll have to

ask him when I see him later.'

'Well, he'd better get a move on if he hasn't,' said Mr Challis, frowning. 'He's running out of time. I should think they'll be selling like hot cakes now...'

That was what I was worried about. I went to meet Dad from work again, and asked him whether he'd gone to the ticket office yet. Of course he hadn't, and my heart sank when I realized this.

'Relax, Gary,' he said, smiling. We were sitting on a park bench with an ice cream each which Dad had bought from a van at the park gates. 'We're not in the final yet – we've still got to face Portugal in the semi-final, and they're good.'

Dad was right. Everybody was talking about Portugal after their comeback against North Korea, and especially their star player, Eusébio, 'The Black Pearl'. The papers were saying he was brilliant, perhaps even as good as the great Pelé himself.

'But Dad, it will probably be too late if you wait till after the semi-final!' I said. Then I told him what Mr Challis had told me. Dad listened, and stopped smiling.

'Ah, well, we might have a problem,' he said. 'I can't just take the day off to go to Wembley. I'll lose a day's pay if I do, and I can't afford that at the moment...'

'So why did you promise that you'd get tickets to the final?' I said. 'They probably cost a lot, and it sounds as if you won't have enough money for them anyway.'

'Have a bit of faith, Gary,' said Dad, frowning at me. 'I'm sure I'll be able to sort something out. And it won't be the end of the world even if I don't, will it?'

'It might be, Dad,' I said. He gave me a funny look, but I turned away.

Then I got on my bike and rode home, pedalling furiously.

West Germany beat the Soviet Union in the other semi-final on the Monday, so we knew who we would have to face if we could get past Portugal. I thought the Germans looked scarily good – they had a great midfield player called Beckenbauer who seemed to dominate the whole game and I didn't know if we had anybody who could match that. Some of their other players – Overath, Seeler, Haller – were nifty too, and I was sure they would be hard to beat.

The Portugal game was on Tuesday evening, and Dad was dead on time again. 'You ready for this, Gary?' he asked. 'It could be the game of the tournament.'

'I suppose so,' I said, shrugging. Mum gave me a sharp look and frowned, so she'd probably guessed I wasn't happy with Dad. In fact at that moment I wasn't sure how I felt. Dad hadn't seemed too bothered by the idea of breaking his promise. But I also thought that maybe I should do as he asked and have a bit of faith in him. There was still time, after all, and the promise wouldn't matter if we didn't beat Portugal…

If anything I felt even more twitchy

and nervous before the semi-final than before the Argentina game, and Portugal looked dangerous right from the kick-off. But England played well too, and the Wembley crowd really got behind the lads. The TV commentator said there were more than 90,000 fans in the stadium, and every single one of them seemed to be clapping and chanting 'ENGLAND! ENGLAND!'

Portugal had a few excellent players – Simões and Torres especially – but of course Eusébio was the greatest threat. I could feel my heart hammering away each time he got the ball, although I began to realize that we might not have to worry – Alf Ramsey had clearly ordered Nobby Stiles to man-mark Eusébio, and he did an amazing job. Eusébio must have thought that he'd grown a second shadow.

I didn't properly relax until we took the lead. Roger Hunt ran on to a long ball from the back and Portugal's keeper got to it first, kicking it out of the area – but only as far as Bobby Charlton, who coolly slid the ball into the goal! The crowd erupted, and so did we – even Mum! The Portuguese came at us again, but Bobby Charlton broke their hearts with another great goal 11 minutes from the end.

It wasn't all easy after that. Gordon Banks had to pull off a brilliant save to keep out a Eusébio shot. Then Jack Charlton stopped a certain Portuguese goal by handling the ball on the line, and Eusébio stepped up to hammer home the penalty which had been given. But the final whistle went at last and the crowd roared. England had beaten one of the best teams in the tournament to make it through to the final of the World Cup! Dad, Susan and I jumped up and danced and hugged each other while Mum looked on, laughing. It was a moment I'd never forget.

So one of the two things that had to happen to bring my parents back together was in the bag. But however good I felt about that, I was still worried. What about the tickets for the final? I didn't dare ask Dad about them, but then he surprised me.

'I've decided I'll take the day off tomorrow after all, Gary,' he said when he was leaving. Mum had already taken Susan up to bed, and Dad and I were at the front door saying goodbye. 'I'll try to get up to the Wembley ticket office as early as possible.'

'That's great, Dad!' I said, and we smiled at each other. That night in bed I crossed my fingers and dreamed about how amazing it would be if Dad got the tickets.

But dreams don't often come true, do they?

CHAPTER SEVEN

Dad phoned early on the Wednesday evening to give me the bad news. Mum answered when the phone rang, then handed the receiver to me.

'I'm sorry, Gary,' Dad said. 'I swear I got there before nine, but the queue at the ticket office must have been a mile long. There were only a few tickets left and they went very quickly. I don't know what else I can do now.'

Mum was still there, looking at me. 'What's he saying?' she mouthed silently, but I ignored her. 'Er… okay, Dad,' I murmured. 'That's fine. Talk to you tomorrow.'

Dad was still speaking, but I quickly put down the receiver. 'Well?' said Mum. She had her arms folded and one eyebrow raised. 'Has your dad kept his promise?'

I stared at her for an instant, my mind racing. I had a feeling that if I told her the truth then that would be it as far as them getting back together was concerned.

'He's still working on it,' I eventually replied. Now Mum sighed and shook her head.

'Nice try, Gary,' she said. 'But I'm not convinced. I was really prepared to give your dad another chance for all our sakes, but don't say I didn't warn you. I hope you're not too upset – you can always watch it on TV, like the other games…'

I spent the rest of the evening lying on my bed. *Maybe I should just give up,* I thought. *Maybe my parents weren't meant to get back together.* But then I caught sight of the picture on one of my walls, a team shot of the England squad that I'd cut out of a comic. There they all were in their white England kit staring at me, and I realized none of them had ever given up – not Bobby Moore or Jack or Bobby Charlton or George Cohen or Alan Ball or Geoff Hurst – and certainly not Nobby Stiles.

So I decided I wasn't going to give up either. There had to be something I could do, some way of making sure that Dad got hold of a couple of final tickets…

I lay awake for most of the next two nights brooding about it, but I didn't come up with anything. On Friday morning morning I met Colin and John. We often hang around with each other in the school holidays – Nan looks after Susan, and Mum likes me to get out of the house and keep myself entertained. So my mates and I usually ride round on our bikes, or go to the park to play football, as we did that day. I'd told Colin and John about my dad and his promise, and now I asked them if they had any ideas.

'Has your dad thought about trying to get tickets from a tout?' said Colin.

It was a hot sunny day, and we were sitting in the shade of a big old elm tree getting our breath back. 'I doubt it,' I said. 'I don't think he likes them much.'

I'd only found out what a ticket tout was earlier that year – they were people who bought up tickets for big games, then sold them at a profit. Not many Crystal Palace games sold out, so touts didn't often come to our ground at Selhurst Park. But they'd been there when we'd drawn Arsenal in the FA Cup – tickets for that game were as scarce as gold dust. We'd already got ours, and when Dad had seen the touts selling tickets outside the ground he'd been angry. He said they weren't supposed to do it, not least because it stopped the real fans getting tickets at prices they could afford.

'Colin's right,' said John. 'That's the only way you'll get any tickets now.'

I really didn't like the idea. But when I thought about it, I remembered another old phrase my grandad sometimes used – 'beggars can't be choosers'. I knew it would be wrong to get the tickets from a tout, but I didn't really have a lot of choice. There was another problem as well – I knew that Dad would refuse to have anything to do with a ticket tout, so it looked as if I'd have to find one and buy the tickets all by myself. But how was I going to do that? The final was tomorrow! I couldn't leave it until then and hope to find a tout outside Wembley, could I?

Suddenly I remembered that I knew someone who might be able to help me. Someone who had quite a few dodgy mates – and who had said he owed me a favour…

Half an hour later I was knocking on Billy Jackson's door.

'A couple of tickets for the World Cup Final,' Billy murmured, rubbing his chin and frowning at me. 'You don't want much, do you? That could be dead tricky.'

We were at the table in Billy's kitchen. Scruffy was on his master's knee and the little dog had seemed pleased to see me, at least judging from the way he had bounced up and down and licked my hands when Billy had let me into the house. So far Billy hadn't been quite so friendly, and I was beginning to wonder if I'd made a mistake.

'Er... I'm not expecting to get them for free, of course,' I said hurriedly. 'I'd be happy to pay for them. I've brought all my savings – I've got over eight quid...'

In fact I had eight pounds, three shillings and fourpence. I'd run all the way home and emptied my piggy bank before I'd come to Billy's house.

Now I pulled it all out of my pockets and piled it up on the table, the coins on top of the notes.

'Yeah, well, I don't think that's going to do it,' said Billy, shaking his head at the heap of money. 'Touts will be after top dollar for a pair of tickets like that…' My heart sank, and Scruffy whined and looked at me with sad eyes, then up at his master. 'All right, Scruffy, don't get worked up, I know I owe him a favour,' said Billy. He swept the money off the table and into the pocket of his jeans. 'I can't promise anything, but I'll see what I can do, okay? Come back later this afternoon…'

It seemed like the longest day of my life. I went home, then to the park with Colin and John again, but I really couldn't concentrate on anything. So I ended up at Billy's house before three o'clock and just hung around outside, waiting. Billy arrived a little after four, strolling down the road with Scruffy on his lead. I tried to tell from Billy's face whether he'd done what I asked, and it was impossible. But I was in luck.

'Here you are,' said Billy, handing me an envelope. 'I got them from a bloke my dad knows. He wanted a lot more than eight quid, though. You'd have thought they were for the Royal Box. So we had to do a bit of persuading, didn't we, Scruffy?'

I decided it was probably best not to ask what he meant by 'a bit of persuading'. As far as I was concerned, the less I knew the better. I opened the envelope and pulled out both tickets.

They were green and surprisingly flimsy, but they seemed to give off a kind of golden glow. They were the most wonderful things I'd ever seen.

'Thanks, Billy,' I said, my voice almost breaking. 'You're a real mate.'

Then I jumped on my bike and rode off to meet Dad from work.

CHAPTER EIGHT

Dad was surprised, to say the least. 'Let me get this straight, Gary,' he said, frowning. 'You asked one of the most notorious thugs on the estate to buy you two tickets for the final from a tout. I'm so angry I don't even know where to start. What on earth were you thinking? They're dangerous people and you could have got into all sorts of bother…'

We were sitting on the same park bench where we'd eaten our ice creams a couple of days earlier. I'd been hoping Dad would simply be grateful to me for getting the tickets, but of course I'd been totally fooling myself. He had lost his temper as soon as

I'd told him about them. Then he had gone on and on about how evil touts were, and how he could never, ever use a ticket that had been bought from one, and how the tickets I'd got might even be fake – I hadn't thought of that. But then suddenly I felt pretty cross too. There had been a very good reason for what I'd done.

'I was thinking… that I just want you and Mum to get back together,' I said.

'Whoa there, hang on a minute,' said Dad. His frown had vanished, and now he was looking confused. 'I don't understand – I would do anything to persuade your mum to take me back, but what has that got to do with these tickets?'

'Mum knows you promised to get them,' I said, shrugging. 'I told her.'

'Is that right?' Dad said quietly. 'I can just imagine her reaction to that.'

‘Yeah, well, she said that you always break your promises, and that’s why she kicked you out. She also said she’d take you back if you started keeping them. But you didn’t seem to care whether you kept your promise about the tickets…’

I had to stop talking then. I was beginning to feel choked up and I didn’t want to cry, not there in the park. I think Dad was upset up too. He certainly didn’t say much for a while, he just stared at me with a guilty expression on his face.

‘So you decided to sort things out yourself,’ he said at last. ‘But how did you even know Billy Jackson in the first place? We’ve always told you to steer well clear of anybody like him. And where did you find the money to pay for the tickets?’

I explained the whole story, and Dad listened without interrupting.

'I'm very impressed, Gary,' he said when I'd finished. Then he sighed, and his shoulders slumped just like Mum's had when she'd been talking about him. 'You've been very clever… but it's not going to work, is it? *You* were the one who bought the tickets, not me. So your mum will know that I didn't keep my promise to you after all, and that's only going to make things worse.'

He was right, of course, but I'd already worked out the solution and I just needed Dad to go along with it. 'We don't have to tell her the truth, do we?' I said. 'We could tell her you did get the tickets.'

'I don't know about that, Gary… it seems a bit dodgy to me,' said Dad, shaking his head. 'I might have let your poor mum down in all sorts of ways, but I've never deliberately lied to her, not once. And I'm not sure I want to start now.'

'Didn't you just say you would do anything to persuade her to take you back? Besides, we're talking about seeing England play in the World Cup Final…'

Dad sat there trying to look stern, but I could tell he was beginning to weaken. I had my fingers crossed on both hands, and hoped he would see sense. I was desperate for my plan to work – I wanted to be at that final so much, and I wanted my parents to get back together even more. Everything depended on what Dad said next.

All right, Gary,' he murmured eventually. 'I'll go along with it, on one condition. You have to make me a promise – that you'll never, ever do anything like this again.'

'Cross my heart and hope to die, Dad,' I said, looking him in the eyes.

Then I rode home on my bike, smiling all the way.

Dad phoned later that evening, and I made sure I got to the phone first. I had to pretend that I didn't know we already had the tickets, which wasn't difficult. But I didn't have to pretend to be excited about going to the game – the feeling was like waiting for all my birthdays and Christmas to arrive together. Mind you, I was a bit worried too – what if England lost?

Mum was surprised, but I could tell she was secretly pleased as well. She even asked to speak to Dad on the phone – 'to sort out the arrangements for tomorrow,' she said. They talked for quite a while, and there was no arguing or shouting.

'So can Dad move back in, then?' I asked as soon as Mum put the phone down. 'He kept his promise to get the tickets, and you said that if he did...'

'I don't need you to remind me what I

said, Gary. It's early days yet, so let's see what happens, shall we? Now come and eat your dinner before it gets cold.'

But she was smiling, and that evening she seemed happier than she had been for ages. I watched the BBC's World Cup Report on TV after dinner – there were experts talking about the final, as well as interviews with some of the players and Alf Ramsey. They all said the Germans would be hard to beat, but also that we had a good chance. There was even talk of Geoff Hurst being dropped and Greaves making a comeback to the team. It seemed like a good thing, although to be honest I thought Hurst had played really well. So that was something else to worry about...

It was really hard to sleep that night, as I couldn't stop thinking about what an amazing day it was going to be tomorrow.

I thought a lot about Mum and Dad and Susan and me too. It was going to be so good for us all to be together again as a family…

I dozed off in the end, but woke up early. I was up, dressed and eating a bowl of Rice Krispies well before seven o'clock. Dad wasn't coming for me till ten.

I thought the hands of the clock would never reach the right place, but they did at last. I was looking out of the front room window so I saw Dad arrive. I ran to the front door and opened it before he had a chance to ring the bell. I would have dragged him off without even letting him come in, but he wanted to say hello to Susan. And to Mum, who was standing in the hall with a big smile on her face.

'Morning, Barbara,' said Dad. 'You're looking particularly lovely today.'

'Oh, stop it,' said Mum. 'You can't get round me like that, you know.'

I wasn't so sure. Mum was smiling even more now. I rolled my eyes at Susan, and my sister smiled. But our parents only had eyes for each other.

'I'm not trying to get round you,' said Dad. 'But I do think we should talk. There are a lot of things I need to say to you, stuff I should have said before—'

'Er… could you leave that for later?' I interrupted. 'I'd really like to get going.'

I was keener than ever for us to leave now. I wanted to get to the final, but I was also worried about the look on Dad's face. All of a sudden he seemed very serious, and I didn't want him to say anything that might give away our secret.

'What? Oh, right,' Dad said. 'See you later, then. Look out for us on TV!'

Mum and Susan waved to us from the door as we set off down the road.

We were on our way to Wembley for the World Cup Final!

CHAPTER NINE

We caught a train into central London, and when we arrived at Charing Cross station we went to have a look at what was happening in Trafalgar Square. It was raining, but the square was full of football fans all the same, with lots of people waving Union Jacks and chanting 'ENGLAND!'. A couple of hundred German fans were there too, singing songs and waving their own flags. Everyone seemed very friendly.

We had an early lunch in a Wimpy Bar in Leicester Square. I had a hamburger and chips and a banana milkshake, and Dad had the same. I like hamburgers even more than I like sausages, so I was feeling pretty cheerful. Dad, however, looked a bit, well… moody. He kept sighing and staring out of the window, and he hardly ate any of his food, either. I had to finish it off for him, which wasn't a problem. I wondered if he was feeling nervous about the game – I certainly was.

Eventually Dad said we ought to make a move, so we headed for the tube. It's quite a long journey from the West End to Wembley, and the train was packed. More people got on at every stop, and I realized they were probably all going to Wembley too. At Wembley Park station we set off for the stadium as part of a huge, happy crowd. Before long I could see the stadium's famous twin towers, and I felt as if I were walking into a film or a story. The whole thing felt totally unreal.

Soon we arrived at the turnstiles and went through. I had a brief moment of panic when Dad handed over the tickets – what if they were fake after all? But they weren't, and then we were in.

The stadium was enormous, much bigger than Selhurst Park, which was the only other ground I'd ever been to. Dad bought me a programme, and we went to find our seats.

That took a long time – they were in the North Stand, right on the halfway line, just above the exit of the tunnel the players would use to get from the changing rooms to the pitch, and only a few rows below the Royal Box.

'Blimey!' Dad said. 'Billy Jackson has done you proud, Gary. These are some of the best seats in the stadium! I can't believe he got them for just eight quid…'

I didn't say a word. I was too busy

looking around, taking everything in as the stadium started to fill up, the excited buzz of the crowd echoing off the stands. The pitch looked even better than I'd thought it would. It was bright green and incredibly smooth, the line markings crisp and white, the tiny corner flags fluttering. The rain had finally stopped, and although the sky was still cloudy the sun was beginning to break through.

There was still a while to go before the kick-off and the time seemed to pass incredibly slowly. A military band marched up and down playing boring old songs and, just when I thought I might explode with impatience, the teams ran out of the tunnel. The whole crowd roared and the noise was almost deafening – we found out later more than 97,000 people were watching. Most were English and waving Union Jacks, but there was a small section of German fans at one end of the stadium.

The Queen had arrived and the players of both teams lined up on the pitch to meet her. The Germans must have got first choice as far as kit was concerned – they were in their usual short-sleeved white shirts and black shorts. England were wearing long-sleeved red shirts and white shorts, which seemed strange as I was used to seeing them in white. I had to tell myself it didn't matter, but it made me uneasy.

I was a bit worried about something else too. 'Do you think Jimmy Greaves should be playing, Dad?' I said. Alf Ramsey had decided to leave him out of the team even though he was fit again. Some people were already saying it was a big mistake.

'Probably best not to break up a winning team,' said Dad. 'I mean, who would Ramsey leave out for him? Hurst and Hunt have both been playing well…'

At last, the two captains – Bobby Moore and Uwe Seeler – met in the centre circle with the referee and the linesmen to shake hands and do the coin toss. I think Bobby Moore won – he chose which end was to be England's in the first half, at any rate. That meant the Germans would kick off. The teams took up their positions and the crowd noise began to build with chants of 'ENGLAND! ENGLAND! ENGLAND!'

It was three o'clock on the afternoon of July 30th 1966, and suddenly I found myself thinking this could turn out to be the best day of my life, or the worst.

In more ways than one.

Things were pretty evenly balanced in the first few moments of the game. The Germans played neat football and looked dangerous when they broke out of defence. But our defence was solid, Bobby Moore like a rock at its heart. I felt nervous, of course, but I began to settle down and tried to enjoy the game – all the passing and running - but my nerves made that impossible.

Then in the twelfth minute one of the German midfielders hit a hopeful ball in the general direction of our area. For some reason our full-back Ray Wilson jumped to head it away instead of letting it go harmlessly out of play, and the ball fell to another German midfielder, Helmut Haller. He controlled it – and struck it past Gordon Banks into the goal. England were one-nil down.

The crowd groaned and the England players looked stunned. I was devastated and I put my head in my hands, convinced I'd just seen the first of a whole flood of German goals.

'Chin up, Gary,' said Dad, squeezing my shoulder. 'It's not over yet.'

He was right, of course, and we came straight back at the Germans. The crowd got behind the team and I could see now why everybody said Bobby Moore was such a fantastic captain – he made lots of great tackles, sprayed amazing passes from defence and encouraged his team-mates. It all paid off. A few moments later Moore was fouled just inside the German half, and took the free kick himself. He hit a perfect long ball to Geoff Hurst, who jumped above all the German defenders and nodded the ball past their keeper.

England had equalized! Dad and I leapt to our feet and the crowd roared.

Nothing quite so dramatic happened for the rest of the half. There was plenty of incident, lots of shots on goal, corners, fouls and free kicks, but neither side could dominate the other. So far Beckenbauer hadn't been much of a threat, which I was relieved about – he seemed to be trying to mark Bobby Charlton out of the game, and that tactic wasn't working. The German striker Siggi Held looked pretty dangerous, though.

The second half was much the same, with both sides testing each other but too nervous to do anything really risky. The crowd got louder and louder, and I shouted myself hoarse. We were all willing England on, trying to help the players with our voices. It seemed to work – as the game wore on I could see that we were becoming the strongest side. We just looked fitter and more confident than the Germans.

Eventually Alan Ball took a corner. Geoff Hurst reached the ball first and hit a great shot, but it got lost in a tangle of players. For a second I couldn't make out what was happening… then the ball bobbed out again and Martin Peters blasted it into the German goal! England were leading by two goals to one!

'How much longer is there, Dad?' I asked. I just wanted it to be over now that we were ahead.

'Twelve minutes, maybe some injury time,' said Dad. 'We're nearly there…'

The clock ticked on, but those twelve minutes seemed to go on forever and I could barely bring myself to watch. Then, right at the end of the game, the Germans were given a free kick a few yards outside our box. The ball was hit low into the area. Boots flailed at it, but then a German player – Wolfgang Weber – scored.

It was two-all, and the referee blew his whistle for full time.

CHAPTER TEN

The Wembley crowd groaned even more loudly than before. We had been so close to winning the World Cup, but it had been snatched from us! Now the lads would have to play half an hour of extra time, fifteen minutes each way.

'How are they going to do it, Dad?' I said. 'They look totally worn out.'

Both sets of players had stayed on the pitch. Most of the Germans were sitting down, and a couple of the England players were too. But Alf Ramsey walked out and got the team to gather round him. I read all the newspapers the next day, so I knew what he said – he was interviewed after the game and told the reporters. He didn't rant and rave like a lot of managers would have done – he spoke very quietly.

'You've won the World Cup once,' he said. 'Now go out and win it again.'

As everyone said afterwards, it was probably the cleverest thing he did in the whole World Cup. The England players were tired, and some of them had their socks rolled down as if it were already over. But they were the much better side in the first half of extra time. The crowd got even louder, and I can't imagine what it must have felt like to be a German player out on that pitch. I think they were incredibly brave just to keep going.

England piled on the pressure and eventually it paid off. Nobby Stiles thumped a long pass down the right wing for Alan Ball to chase. He beat a German defender, then knocked a low cross towards Geoff Hurst in the German penalty area. Hurst controlled the ball and then whacked it over the keeper's head. The ball hit the underside of the bar, bounced very close to the goal line and came spinning out again.

The England team raised their arms and the crowd roared 'GOAL!' But the German players protested, several of them running up to the referee. The crowd grew quiet as the referee ran over to consult with the linesman. He nodded and the referee gave the goal. The crowd went wild – we were three-two up! But some of the Germans followed the referee back to the centre circle, arguing with him all the way.

'Do you think it was a goal, Dad?' I said, turning to him. 'They don't.'

'It really doesn't matter a hoot what they think,' said Dad, grinning at me.

'The referee's in charge, and he gave it. That's all anybody needs to know.'

There were still twenty minutes of extra time to go, and each one of them was total agony. You could feel the incredible tension in the stadium, every England fan willing the Germans not to equalize, all of us desperate to hear the final whistle. Then it seemed at last as if it were about to happen. The referee raised his whistle and a few people ran onto the pitch to celebrate, even though the game wasn't officially over yet. But there was one more surprise to come.

The Germans had thrown everything at us, and they were making one last attack. Then Bobby Moore cut out a cross and brought the ball forward. He saw Geoff Hurst just inside the German half and passed to him… a perfect ball! Hurst turned and went past a German defender and took the ball on towards the opposition goal. Another German defender was moving in to try and make a tackle, but he was too late.

Of course, I was there at Wembley, so I wasn't watching the game on the TV. But I heard afterwards what the BBC commentator said at this point, as it's probably the most famous quote ever from a football commentator. 'Some people are on the pitch, they think it's all over...' he announced, and at that moment Hurst blasted the ball into the back of the German net, his third goal in the final. 'It is now!'

The referee blew his whistle and the game ended. The crowd roared, but I turned and hugged my dad, and we jumped up and down and hugged each other and yelled and screamed like crazy. England had won the World Cup four-two! I could hardly believe my wish had come true...

After a while, the teams went up to the Royal Box to collect their medals, the Germans first. Our seats were beside the stairs, so the players were very close as they walked past. I even patted Bobby Moore on the back, and he turned to smile at me. It was a special moment for me, one I knew I would remember forever. He wiped his hands on his shorts before the Queen presented him with his medal and the World Cup.

He raised the Cup to the crowd, and we roared one last time.

The England players stayed on the pitch for ages – I have a feeling they didn't want their day to end. I knew there would be some other things I would never forget – Bobby Moore sitting on the shoulders of his team-mates, Bobby Charlton crying, Nobby Stiles giving everyone a toothless grin and doing a little dance with the cup on his head.

The warm sun shone down on everybody as if it were as happy as the rest of us.

'Come on, Gary,' Dad said at last. 'I think

we'd better be making tracks.'

I took a last look at the emptying stadium. I didn't want it to end either. It was a magical place and part of me wanted to stay there forever.

But I turned around at last and we headed for home.

It was a bit of a wild journey. Everyone on our tube train was singing and chanting, and an older man told me he hadn't seen anything like it since May 8th 1945, the day the war had ended. We got off in the West End and went to have a look at what was happening in Trafalgar Square. It was even more packed than before, and now hundreds of people were in the fountains, cheering and waving Union Jacks.

The only person who didn't seem ecstatic, in fact, was Dad. He'd been all right at the game, but the closer we got to home, the more moody he became. I couldn't understand it. He was very quiet as we walked from the station to our house, and anyone who didn't know the result might have thought we'd just lost the World Cup, not won it. I hoped he would cheer up once we were indoors.

He didn't, though. Mum and Susan were all smiles and laughter, asking us about the game and saying they hadn't been able to see us on TV. Dad just stood there looking glum, and eventually the rest of us fell silent and turned to him.

'Are you all right, Mike?' said Mum at last. 'You don't seem too happy.'

'Well, that's because I'm not,' Dad said. 'I have a confession to make...'

Oh no, don't do this, Dad, I thought. But it was too late. Dad told Mum that he hadn't kept his promise and that I had been the one who had got the tickets.

'I thought there was something dodgy going on,' said Mum. Her smile had vanished and she looked unhappy again. 'When will you learn, Mike?'

'I have learned, Barbara,' said Dad, taking her hand. Susan and I stood between them, looking from one to the other as they spoke as if we were at a tennis match. 'I know I've let you down, but now I see that I've got to change. Look at what our son did to try and bring us together! We owe it to our lovely kids to make a go of it, and I know that's up to me. What do you say, sweetheart? Will you take me back?'

'Oh, go on, Mum,' I couldn't resist adding. 'You know you want to. And if you do, I'm pretty sure Dad will promise never to make promises he can't keep again – that's right, isn't it, Dad?'

Dad laughed, and Mum did too. Then she nodded slowly and they hugged each other, and pulled me and Susan into the hug too. So I knew it was going to be okay.

I felt so good it was as if I'd just won the World Cup all by myself.